MW01098946

MY FIRST
BOOK OF
POEMS

This edition © Ward Lock Limited
1989

First published in the U.S. in
1989 by Ideals Publishing Corporation,
Nashville, Tennessee.

ISBN 0-8249-8384-X

Printed and bound in Czechoslovakia

MY FIRST
BOOK OF
POEMS

Illustrated by Margaret Tarrant

IDEALS CHILDREN'S BOOKS
Nashville, Tennessee

THE LAND OF COUNTERPANE

When I was sick and lay a-bed,
I had two pillows at my head,
And all my toys beside me lay
To keep me happy all the day.

And sometimes for an hour or so
I watched my leaden soldiers go,
With different uniforms and drills,
Among the bedclothes, through the hills;

And sometimes sent my ships in fleets
All up and down among the sheets;
Or brought my trees and houses out,
And planted cities all about.

I was the giant great and still
That sits upon the pillow-hill,
And sees before him, dale and plain,
The pleasant land of counterpane.

Robert Louis Stevenson

COME UNTO THESE YELLOW SANDS

Come unto these yellow sands,
And then take hands:
Curtsied when you have and kiss'd,
The wild waves whist,
Foot it featly here and there;
And, sweet sprites, the burden bear.
Hark, hark!
Bow wow
The watch-dogs bark:
Bow wow
Hark, hark! I hear
The strain of strutting chanticleer
Cry, *Cock-a-diddle-dow*.

William Shakespeare

CHILD'S SONG IN
SPRING

The silver birch is a dainty lady,
    She wears a satin gown;
The elm tree makes the old churchyard shady,
    He will not live in town.

The English oak is a sturdy fellow,
    He gets his green coat late;
The willow is smart in a suit of yellow,
    While the brown beech trees wait.

Such a gay green gown God gives the larches—
    As green as He is good!
The hazels hold up their arms for arches
    When Spring rides through the wood.

The chestnut's proud and the lilac's pretty,
    The poplar's gentle and tall,
But the plane tree is kind to the poor dull city—
    I love him best of all!

F. Nesbit

BUBBLE-BLOWING

Our plot is small, but sunny limes
   Shut out all cares and troubles;
And there my little girl at times
   And I sit blowing bubbles.

They glide, they dart, they soar, they break.
   Oh, joyous little daughter,
What lovely coloured worlds we make,
   What crystal flowers of water!

One, green and rosy, slowly drops;
   One soars and shines a minute,
And carries to the lime tree tops
   Our home, reflected in it.

To her enchanted with the gleam,
   The glamour and the glory,
The bubble home's a home of dream,
   And I must tell its story.

William Canton

WYNKEN, BLYNKEN, AND NOD

Wynken, Blynken, and Nod one night
  Sailed off in a wooden shoe,—
Sailed on a river of crystal light
  Into a sea of dew.
"Where are you going, and what do you wish?"
  The old moon asked the three.
"We have come to fish for the herring fish
  That live in this beautiful sea;
Nets of silver and gold have we,"

      Said Wynken,
      Blynken,
      And Nod.

continued

The old moon laughed and sang a song,
    As they rocked in the wooden shoe;
And the wind that sped them all night long
    Ruffled the waves of dew.
The little stars were the herring fish
    That lived in the beautiful sea—
"Now cast your nets wherever you wish,
    Never afeared are we!"
So cried the stars to the fishermen three:

Wynken,
Blynken,
And Nod.

All night long their nets they threw
    For the fish in the twinkling foam,
Then down from the sky came the wooden
        shoe,
    Bringing the fishermen home;
'Twas all so pretty a sail, it seemed
    As if it could not be;

And some folk thought 'twas a dream they'd
    dreamed
   Of sailing that beautiful sea—
But I shall name you the fishermen three:

        Wynken,
        Blynken,
        And Nod.

Wynken and Blynken are two little eyes,
   And Nod is a little head,
And the wooden shoe that sailed the skies
   Is a wee one's trundle bed;
So shut your eyes while Mother sings
   Of wonderful sights that be,
And you shall see the beautiful things,
   As you rock in the misty sea,
Where the old shoe rocked the
    fishermen three—
   Wynken, Blynken, and Nod.

                    Eugene Field

A PATTERN BABY

When people come to call and tell
About their babies, dear me, well—
I sit and listen all the while
And smile myself a little smile.
If mine were like some people's, there,
I would not keep her, I declare!
Their babies scream and cry and fret,
Won't eat or sleep, while my dear pet
She *never* cries; she'll stay for hours
Just looking at the birds and flowers.
The sweetest little cot has she,
All pink and white, as smart can be.
And when at night I lay her in it
She shuts her eyes in half a minute.
That all the babies in the city
Are not like mine I think a pity.
The only thing is, mine won't grow—
She is a baby doll, you know.

E. A. Mayo

MUSTARD AND CRESS

Elizabeth, my cousin, is the sweetest
   little girl,
From her eyes like dark blue pansies to her
   tiniest golden curl;
I do not use her great long name, but simply
   call her Bess,
And yesterday I planted her in mustard and
   in cress.

My garden is so narrow that there's very little
   room,
But I'd rather have her name than get a
   hollyhock to bloom;
And before she comes to visit us, with
   Charley and with Jess,
She'll pop up green and bonny out of mustard
   and of cress.

Norman Gale

A BOY'S SONG

Where the pools are bright and deep,
Where the grey trout lies asleep,
Up the river and over the lea,
That's the way for Billy and me.

Where the hazel bank is steepest,
Where the shadow falls the deepest,
Where the clustering nuts fall free,
That's the way for Billy and me.

Why the boys should drive away
Little sweet maidens from the play,
Or love to banter and fight so well,
That's the thing I never could tell.

But this I know, I love to play
Through the meadow, among the hay;
Up the water and over the lea,
That's the way for Billy and me.

James Hogg

THE DREAM OF A BOY WHO LIVED AT NINE-ELMS

Nine grenadiers, with bayonets in their guns;
Nine bakers' baskets, with hot cross buns;
Nine brown elephants, standing in a row;
Nine new velocipedes, good ones to go;
Nine knickerbocker suits, with buttons
   all complete;
Nine pairs of skates, with straps for the feet;
Nine clever conjurers eating hot coals;
Nine sturdy mountaineers leaping on
   their poles;
Nine little drummer boys beating on
   their drums;
Nine fat aldermen sitting on their thumbs;
Nine new knockers to our front door;
Nine new neighbours that I never saw before;
Nine times running I dreamt it all plain;
With bread and cheese for supper I could
   dream it all again.
               William Brighty Rands

22

23

THE ROCK-A-BY LADY

The Rock-a-by Lady from Hushaby Street
Comes stealing, comes creeping;
The poppies they hang from her head to
    her feet,
And each hath a dream that is tiny
    and fleet—
She bringeth her poppies to you, my sweet,
When she findeth you sleeping!

Would you dream all these dreams that are
    tiny and fleet?
They'll come to you sleeping;
So shut the two eyes that are weary,
    my sweet,
For the Rock-a-by Lady from Hushaby
    Street,
With poppies that hang from her head to
    her feet,
Comes stealing; comes creeping.

Eugene Field

SEVEN TIMES ONE

There's no dew left on the daisies and clover,
　　There's no rain left in heaven:
I've said my "seven times" over and over,
　　Seven times one are seven.

I am old, so old I can write a letter;
　　My birthday lessons are done;
The lambs play always, they know no better;
　　They are only one times one.

O Columbine, open your folded wrapper,
　　Where two twin turtledoves dwell!
O Cuckoopint, toll me the purple clapper
　　That hangs in your clear green bell!

And show me your nest, with the young
　　　ones in it;
　　I will not steal them away;
I am old! You may trust me, linnet, linnet,—
　　I am seven times one today.

Jean Ingelow

OUR VISIT TO THE ZOO

When we went to the Zoo
We saw a gnu,
An elk and a whelk
And a wild emu.

We saw a hare,
And a bear in his lair,
And a seal have a meal
On a high-backed chair.

We saw a snake
That was hardly awake,
And a lion eat meat
They'd forgotten to bake.

We saw a crab and a long-tailed dab,
And we all went home in a taxicab.

Jessie Pope

CATCHING FAIRIES

They're sleeping beneath the roses;
Oh! kiss them before they rise,
And tickle their tiny noses,
And sprinkle the dew on their eyes.
Make haste, make haste;
The fairies are caught,
Make haste.

They'll scatter sweet scents by winking,
With sparks from under their feet;
They'll save us the trouble of thinking,
Their voices will sound so sweet.
Oh stay, oh stay;
They're up and away,
Oh stay!

William Cory

THE LOST DOLL

I once had a sweet little doll, dears,
    The prettiest doll in the world;
Her cheeks were so red and so white, dears,
    And her hair was so charmingly curled.
But I lost my poor little doll, dears,
    As I played in the heath one day;
And I cried for her more than a week, dears;
    But I never could find where she lay.

I found my poor little doll, dears,
    As I played in the heath one day;
Folks say she is terribly changed, dears,
    For her paint is all washed away,
And her arm trodden off by the cows, dears,
    And her hair not the least bit curled:
Yet for old sakes' sake she is still, dears,
    The prettiest doll in the world.

Charles Kingsley

THE LOST DOLL.

A CHILD'S THOUGHT
OF GOD

They say that God lives very high!
But if you look above the pines
You cannot see our God. And why?
And if you dig down in the mines,
You never see Him in the gold,
Though from Him all that's glory shines.

God is so good, He wears a fold
Of heaven and earth across His face,
Like secrets kept, for love untold.
But still I feel that His embrace
Slides down by thrills, through all things made,
Through sight and sound of every place:

As if my tender mother laid
On my shut lids, her kisses' pressure,
Half-waking me at night; and said,
"Who kissed you in the dark, dear guesser?"

Elizabeth Barrett Browning

TARTARY

If I were Lord of Tartary,
　　Myself and me alone,
My bed should be of ivory,
　　Of beaten gold my throne;
And in my court should peacocks flaunt,
And in my forests tigers haunt,
And in my pools great fishes slant
　　Their fins athwart the sun.

If I were Lord of Tartary,
　　Trumpeters every day
To all my meals should summon me,
　　And in my courtyards bray;
And in the evenings lamps should shine
Yellow as honey, red as wine,
While harp and flute and mandoline
　　Made music sweet and gay.

Walter De La Mare

I SAW A SHIP A-SAILING

I saw a ship a-sailing,
    A-sailing on the sea;
And, oh! it was all laden
    With pretty things for thee!

There were comfits in the cabin,
    And apples in the hold;
The sails were all of silk,
    And the masts were made of gold.

Old Rhyme

AUTUMN FIRES

In the other gardens
   And all up the vale,
From the autumn bonfires
   See the smoke trail!

Pleasant summer over
   And all the summer flowers,
The red fire blazes,
   The grey smoke towers.

Sing a song of seasons!
   Something bright in all!
Flowers in the summer,
   Fires in the fall!

Robert Louis Stevenson

THE FIRST OF MAY

The fair maid who, the First of May,
  Goes to the fields at break of day,
And washes in dew from the hawthorn tree,
  Will ever after handsome be.

Old Rhyme

INFANT JOY

"I have no name;
I am but two days old."
—What shall I call thee?
"I happy am;
Joy is my name."
—Sweet joy befall thee!

Pretty joy!
Sweet joy, but two days old;
Sweet joy I call thee:
Thou dost smile:
I sing the while,
Sweet joy befall thee!

William Blake

THE MONTHS

January brings the snow,
Makes our feet and fingers glow.

February brings the rain,
Thaws the frozen lake again.

March brings breezes loud and shrill,
Stirs the dancing daffodil.

April brings the primrose sweet,
Scatters daisies at our feet.

May brings flocks of pretty lambs,
Skipping by their fleecy dams.

June brings tulips, lilies, roses,
Fills the children's hands with posies.

Hot July brings cooling showers,
Apricots and gillyflowers.

August brings the sheaves of corn,
Then the harvest home is borne.   *continued*

Warm September brings the fruit,
Sportsmen then begin to shoot.

Fresh October brings the pheasant,
Then to gather nuts is pleasant.

Dull November brings the blast,
Then the leaves are whirling fast.

Chill December brings the sleet,
Blazing fire and Christmas treat.

Sara Coleridge

OLD MOTHER GOOSE

Old Mother Goose,
  When she wanted to wander
Would ride through the air
  On a very fine gander.

Mother Goose had a house,
  'Twas built in a wood,
Where an owl at the door
  As sentinel stood.

She had a son Jack,
  A plain-looking lad,
He was not very good,
  Nor yet very bad.

She sent him to market,
  A live goose he bought;
"Here, Mother," says he,
  "It will not go for nought."

Old Rhyme

ORANGES AND LEMONS

Fast beneath the archway going
Hurry, hurry—never knowing
   When the arch will stop you!
First there comes the candle-lighting,
Then you will—it's most exciting!—
   Feel the chopper chop you!

Now we're off. Oh, hold on tight there!
Tug away with all your might there!
   Now we've nearly won it!
Lemons break, and red with laughter,
On the ground they're lying after.
   Oranges have done it!

Old Rhyme

PEG TOPS

Oh, people, please mind where you're setting
   your feet,
For peg tops are spinning all over the street,
And if they should tumble, with might and
   with main,
We have all of these tops to get spinning again.

The boys who are big will just give them
   a twirl
And all in a minute you'll see the tops whirl;
But if you are smaller, you have to begin
Quite three times or four times before they
   will spin.

Old Rhyme

A CHINESE NURSERY SONG

The mouse ran up the candlestick,
To eat the grease from off the wick.
When we got up, he could not get down,
But squeaked to waken all the town:
Ma-ma-ma! Ma-ma-ma!

From *"Cradle Songs of Many Nations"*

DAYS OF BIRTH

Monday's child is fair of face,
Tuesday's child is full of grace,
Wednesday's child is full of woe,
Thursday's child has far to go,

Friday's child is loving and giving,
Saturday's child works hard for its living,
But the child that is born on the Sabbath Day
Is fair, and wise, and good, and gay.

Old Rhyme

MONDAY'S CHILD

TUESDAY'S CHILD

WEDNESDAY'S CHILD

THURSDAY'S CHILD

FRIDAY'S CHILD

SATURDAY'S CHILD

SUNDAY'S CHILD

HERE WE GO ROUND THE MULBERRY BUSH

Here we go round the mulberry bush,
 The mulberry bush, the mulberry bush,
Here we go round the mulberry bush,
 So early in the morning.

This is the way we wash our hands,
Wash our hands, wash our hands,
This is the way we wash our hands
 So early in the morning.

This is the way we go to school,
Go to school, go to school,
This is the way we go to school
 So early in the morning.

Old Rhyme

THE <u>PEDLAR'S</u> CARAVAN

I wish I lived in a caravan,
With a horse to drive, like a pedlar-man!
Where he comes from nobody knows,
Or where he goes to, but on he goes!

His caravan has windows two,
And a chimney of tin, that the smoke
   comes through;
He has a wife with a baby brown,
And they go a-riding from town to town.

Chairs to mend, and delft to sell!
He clashes the basins like a bell;
Tea trays, baskets ranged in order,
Plates, with alphabets round the border!

The roads are brown, and the sea is green,
But his house is like a bathing-machine;
The world is round, and he can ride,
Rumble and splash, to the other side!

continued